D1006332

Beauty & the Beast

Retold by Louie Stowell

Illustrated by Victor Tavares

Reading consultant: Alison Kelly
Roehampton University

Contents

Chapter 1

Beauty

There was once a very rich man, named Pierre, who gave his three daughters *everything* they wanted.

"Bring us rubies and silks from the market!" demanded Sophie and Marie, his eldest daughters.

Oh, and a satin dress!

And pearls.

Pierre turned to his youngest daughter. "Don't you want anything, Beauty?" he asked.

4

"May I have a rose?" asked Beauty. "They always seem to die in our garden."

"I wonder why?" said Marie.

"It's a mystery," added Sophie. "And *such* a shame when you love them so."

Pierre waved goodbye to his daughters and galloped away on his sleek white horse.

As he rode, a thick fog filled the air. Pierre couldn't see the path ahead, or even his horse below him.

He went on blindly,
until suddenly...

...the fog rolled back to reveal
a towering castle.
Pierre gasped. "Where am I?"

7

Chapter 2

The Beast

The horse's hooves
clattered up to
the castle gates.
They opened before
him with a
ghostly creak.

Pierre rode into a courtyard. As he raised his hand to knock on the castle door, it swung open.

"Hello?" he called. No one answered. He tried again. "Hello?" But Pierre only heard his own voice, echoing off the stone walls.

Is anybody here?

"What's going on?" he murmured, his heart beating faster. Then a mouth-watering smell made him forget his fear.

Pierre followed his nose to an enormous feast. He sat down, nervously. "Where are the guests?" he said to himself.

A full plate floated over to him
and he cried out in surprise. But he
was cold and starving and the food
smelled so good.

"I hope no one minds," he
thought, picking up a silver fork.

Invisible hands poured him rich,
sweet wine.

Feeling full and tired, Pierre rose from the table. Instantly, a bed appeared before him. Pierre was too exhausted to question it. He just lay down... and fell fast asleep.

He woke in a beautiful bedroom. A pile of clean clothes sat on a seat by the bed. They were just his size.

"I must find the owners and thank them," Pierre thought, and set out to search the castle corridors. Invisible hands opened all the doors, but he couldn't find a single living person anywhere.

"Perhaps everyone's outside?" Pierre wondered.

In the garden, he found a beautiful rosebush. As he sniffed the blooms, he remembered his promise to Beauty.

14

The instant Pierre plucked a
flower, a huge shadow fell over the
rosebushes. He spun around,
clutching the bloom to his chest...

15

...to see a hideous creature before him. Its eyes glittered fiercely. Before Pierre could cry out, it grabbed him and pulled him close to its angry face.

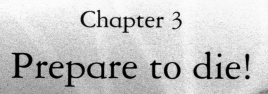

Chapter 3

Prepare to die!

"How dare you steal from the Beast?" demanded the terrifying creature. "I gave you food and shelter, and this is how you repay me? Thief!"

"I'm s-s-sorry," said Pierre, trembling all over.

The Beast glared at him and gave a low growl.

"I'll pay for the flower!" cried Pierre, desperately.

"Yes, you'll pay," said the Beast. "You'll pay with your life!"

"Please don't harm me," begged
Pierre. "I just wanted a rose for
Beauty – for my daughter."

Daughter?

The Beast fixed his burning eyes on Pierre. "I'll let you live if you send Beauty to me. If she refuses, you must return in a week to meet your fate," he declared. "Or I'll come after you!"

"I can't risk Beauty's life," Pierre thought. With a heavy heart, he told the Beast he would return.

Before Pierre left, the Beast put a ruby bridle on the horse's muzzle. "He'll be able to find his way to your home and back," said the Beast. "The bridle will guide him."

"I'm home!"
called Pierre, as
he came down the
path. Beauty ran
to him, smiling.
     "How was the trip?"
     "Fine," said Pierre.
He couldn't bear
to tell her the truth.

As the week passed,
Pierre grew thin and pale.
"What's wrong, Father?"
Beauty asked.
"Nothing," he replied.
"Please don't worry
about me."

That night, Beauty
thought she heard
him crying.

She found him asleep at his desk the next morning, with a letter in front of him. She picked it up and started to read.

Dearest daughters,
When you read this letter
I will have left you forever.
I took a rose from the garden
of a monstrous beast and he
has sworn to kill me unless
I bring him my youngest
daughter. I could never do
that to you, Beauty, so
I have gone in your place.

Farewell,

Your loving Father x x

"Oh no!" cried Beauty. "This is all my fault."

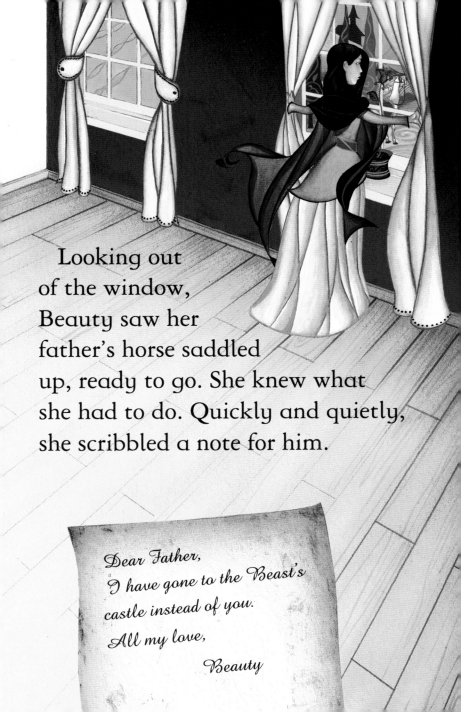

Looking out
of the window,
Beauty saw her
father's horse saddled
up, ready to go. She knew what
she had to do. Quickly and quietly,
she scribbled a note for him.

Dear Father,
I have gone to the Beast's
castle instead of you.
All my love,
Beauty

Her father's horse seemed
to know the way. He galloped
down the twisting paths as if
guided by a magic force.

As the Beast's
castle came into view, Beauty
gripped the reins in fear.

Chapter 4

Beauty and the Beast

First, the castle gates creaked
open before her, then the door to
the castle itself. "This place must
be enchanted," Beauty realized.
She took a deep breath and
stepped inside.

Beauty tiptoed down a long
and dusty corridor until she
found an open door. It led into
a sweet-smelling garden. But as
soon as Beauty stepped into
the sunlight...

...she heard a
terrible growl. "What are
you doing here?" roared the Beast.

"I'm B-b-beauty, Pierre's daughter," she stammered.

"He sent you to die, did he?" the Beast growled. "Coward!"

"Don't say that!" said Beauty. She was so angry she forgot her fear and glared at the Beast.

"You have courage," said the Beast, gazing back at her. As he spoke, Beauty was shocked to see great tears forming in his eyes.

"What's wrong?" she asked.

"Having you here makes me realize – I've been alone for so long," sniffed the Beast.

"Poor Beast," said Beauty, her heart filling with pity. "I'll stay with you, if you like."

The Beast grasped her hand, his eyes shining with hope. "Thank you," he said gruffly.

But you must let my father know I'm safe.

The Beast strode out to the courtyard and tied a note to Pierre's horse, then sent it on its way.

That evening, Beauty and the Beast dined together. The Beast told Beauty a story about a princess who turned a frog into a prince with a kiss.

In return, Beauty told the Beast all about her family and her life. "You're a very good listener," she said. "My sisters always interrupt."

The Beast looked at Beauty very seriously, then knelt before her.

"I know this is sudden," he said in a low voice, "and I know I'm ugly, but... will you marry me?"

33

"I can't," gasped Beauty. "I don't even know you."

"Very well," said the Beast, bowing his head. "Goodnight, Beauty. Your room is next door," he added, and left her alone.

Chapter 5

Beauty explores

Beauty dreamed of home and woke wishing she was there. Then, as she dressed, she saw a mirror by her bed. Peering into it, she was amazed to see her father, eating breakfast back at home.

A magic mirror!

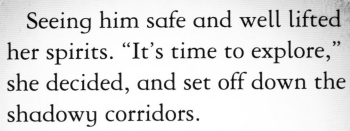

Seeing him safe and well lifted
her spirits. "It's time to explore,"
she decided, and set off down the
shadowy corridors.

In one room she saw fairies
performing a play on an
enchanted stage.

In another, she
found a library with shelves
that seemed to stretch to the sky.
"Here you will find every book in
the world," boomed a voice. "Books
from both the past and the future."

When Beauty went out into
the garden, she saw exotic flowers
and magical animals.

But she didn't see the Beast
all day.

At eight o'clock,
a gong rang for dinner.
The Beast was waiting
for Beauty in the dining
room. "Did you find the
mirror?" he asked, eagerly.
"I loved it. Thank
you," Beauty replied.
After dinner, the
Beast went down
on one knee again.

Marry me,
Beauty.

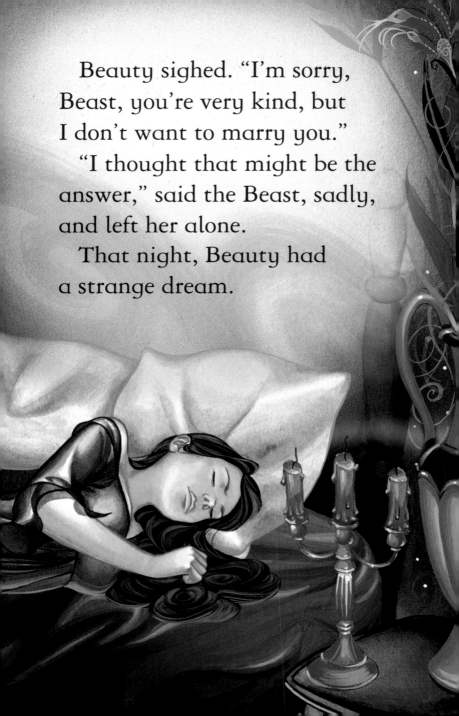

Beauty sighed. "I'm sorry,
Beast, you're very kind, but
I don't want to marry you."

"I thought that might be the
answer," said the Beast, sadly,
and left her alone.

That night, Beauty had
a strange dream.

She was dining with a
handsome prince.

"How can you bear to look at
that ugly Beast?" he asked.

"He's not ugly inside,"
said Beauty.

"But he's a monster,"
said the Prince.

How could anyone
love a beast?

Beauty woke to the sound of birds singing. The Prince from her dream had vanished. "Is that all he was... a dream?" Beauty wondered. She spent the day wandering from room to room. The castle seemed empty without the Beast beside her.

Beauty was trying
to choose a book
from the library,
when she noticed
a portrait.

She couldn't
believe her eyes.
It was the Prince
from her dream.

43

At dinner that evening, she asked the Beast about him. "I dreamed of a prince last night," she said, "and then I saw a painting of him in the library. Do you know who he is?"

"I know him," said the Beast. "But I haven't seen him for years."

For the rest of the meal the Beast refused to talk more about the Prince. After they finished, he asked her to marry him again.

"I like you, but I don't love you," Beauty said softly. "I'm sorry, but I won't marry you."

The Beast sighed and said goodnight.

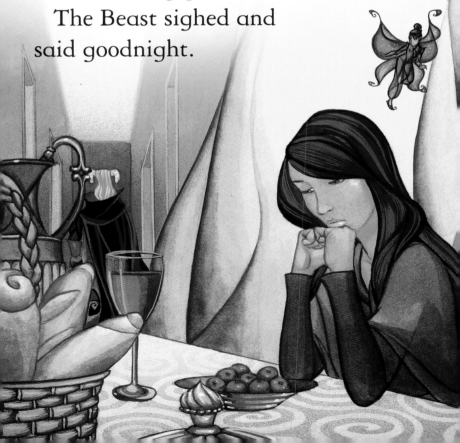

The next morning,
Beauty watched her family
in her mirror. She missed
them more than ever.
At dinner that
evening, she hardly
ate a thing.

"What's the matter?" the Beast
asked her, with a worried frown.

"I'm homesick," said Beauty.

The Beast pulled a ring from
his pocket.

"Oh Beast, I still won't marry
you," she said quickly.

The Beast shook his head. "This
isn't a wedding ring. It's magic. It
will take you back to your father."

47

"But you must promise me you'll
return in two weeks," he went on.
"I promise," said Beauty.
"Oh thank you, Beast!"
"Keep it safe in your pocket.
When you're ready to return,
put the ring on your bedside
table," he told her.

Beauty nodded. She put
on the ring and the room
melted away. She felt
herself falling... falling...
until suddenly she was
standing on solid ground
again. She was back at
home and her father
was staring at her,
open-mouthed.

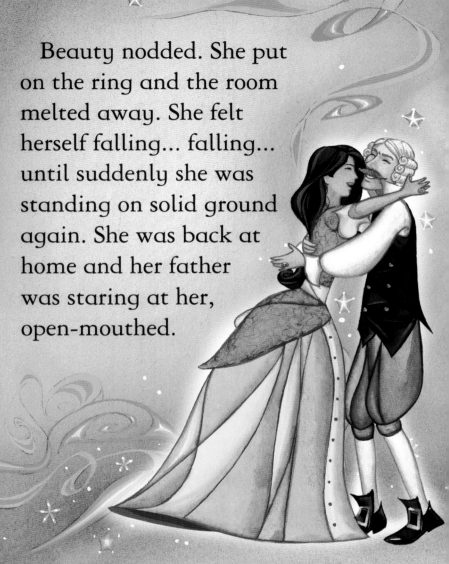

"Oh Father!" she cried, throwing
her arms around him.

Chapter 6

Tricked

The Beast is really very sweet.

Beauty's father was overjoyed to see her... unlike her sisters.

When they heard she had to return in two weeks, they hatched a secret plan.

"If we make her stay longer, the Beast will be angry. With any luck, he might even eat her," said Marie, with a sly smile.

"With little Beauty gone, we'll have Father and his fortune all to ourselves," added Sophie.

So the sisters started being very sweet and loving to Beauty.

Beauty was surprised at the change in them. "They must have really missed me," she thought.

The two weeks flew
by, but Beauty kept
thinking of the Beast.
Was he lonely
without her?

When the time
came for her to
return, her sisters
burst into noisy sobs.

"We can't live without you!"
they howled. "If you loved us,
you'd stay!" said
Sophie, clutching
Beauty's hands.

Reluctantly, Beauty stayed...
until one night, she dreamed she
saw the Beast lying in his garden,
under a rose bush.

Beauty woke with a start.
"Something's wrong," she realized.
"I must go to him."

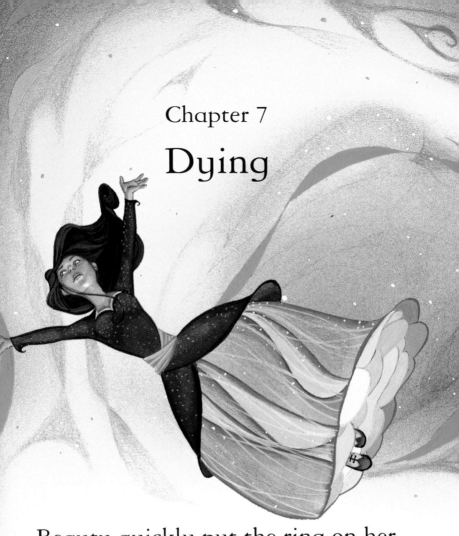

Chapter 7

Dying

Beauty quickly put the ring on her bedside table. A cloud of swirling smoke surrounded her. The next instant, she vanished.

Beauty was back in the garden. The Beast was lying under the rose bush, just as in her dream.

"Beast?" whispered Beauty, kneeling down beside him.

The Beast struggled to open his eyes. "Is that you Beauty?" he asked. "I'm dying."

"No!" cried Beauty, horrified. "Why? What happened?" She stroked his velvety face and kissed him. "You can't die! Please, Beast. I love you. Don't die."

There was a blinding flash and a deafening bang.

The Beast disappeared. A second later, there was another, brighter flash and an even louder bang.

Kneeling before her was a handsome prince.

"You were in my dream... and in the painting!" cried Beauty.

"Who are you? What happened to my Beast?" she asked. Her mind was spinning.

The Prince smiled.

"Many years ago," he explained, "an angry fairy turned me into a Beast because I refused to marry her. Only the love of a beautiful girl could make me human again."

"But why were you dying?" asked Beauty.

"The fairy said if I loved
a girl who did not love me,
I would die of a broken heart,"
the Prince replied.

"You don't need to be afraid,"
said Beauty. "I do love you."

Beauty and the Prince were
married the next day, in a church
filled with roses.

Beauty's sisters left early in bad
tempers. "Why does she get to
marry a prince? It's not fair!"

"Life isn't fair," said a tiny voice.
It was the fairy who had cursed
the prince.

"Your sister broke my spell," she said, "but at least I can give you exactly what you deserve."

"What?" yelped the sisters.

"As you have hearts of stone," the fairy declared, waving her wand, "that's what you'll be... forever!"

Then, feeling much better, she flew off to steal some wedding cake.

Beauty and the Beast was first written down in 1740 by a French woman named Gabrielle de Villeneuve. There have been many different versions since, including a Disney cartoon and a number of novels. This version is based on Villeneuve's story and a retelling from 1756 by another French writer, Marie Le Prince de Beaumont.

Edited by Susanna Davidson
Series editor: Lesley Sims
Designed by Natacha Goransky

This edition first published in 2008 by Usborne Publishing Ltd., Usborne House, 83-85 Saffron Hill, London EC1N 8RT, England. www.usborne.com Copyright © 2008, 2006 Usborne Publishing Ltd.